Almos' A Man

Richard Wright

LOOKING FORWARD

Richard Wright's "Almos'a Man" is about a boy's struggle to be a man. For Dave Sanders that struggle is made more complicated by blackness and poverty. Frustrated by others' refusal to recognize him as an adult, Dave seizes upon a gun to demonstrate his manhood; in doing so, he accidentally kills a mule. Faced with a beating by his father and two years of labor to pay for the mule Jenny, Dave runs, taking with him his symbol of manhood and proving that he is still only almost a man.

WORDS TO WATCH FOR

Here are some words with which you may not be familiar. Next to each is a short definition. Review the words and their meanings before you begin to read.

ooze – to escape; to flow out
elated – joyful; to be extremely happy
reflectively – as if thinking or considering
traces – straps or lines on a harness
gingerly – cautiously; very carefully

3 4 5 6 7 8 PP 17 16 15 14 13 12

Dave struck out across the fields, looking homeward through paling light. Whut's the usa talkin wid em niggers in the field? Anyhow, his mother was putting supper on the table. Them niggers can't understan nothing. One of these days he was going to get a gun and practice shooting, then they can't talk to him as though he were a little boy. He slowed, looking at the ground. Shucks, Ah ain scareda them even ef they are biggern me! Aw, Ah know whut Ahma do. . . . Ahm going by ol Joe's sto n git that Sears Roebuck catlog n look at them guns. Mabbe Ma will lemme buy one when she gits mah pay from ol man Hawkins. Ahma beg her t gimme some money. Ahm ol ernough to hava gun. Ahm seventeen. Almost a man. He strode, felling his long, loose-joint limbs, Shucks, a man oughta hava little gun aftah he done worked hard all day. . . .

He came in sight of Joe's store. A yellow lantern glowed on the front porch. He mounted steps and went through the screen door, hearing it bang behind him. There was a strong smell of coal oil and mackerel fish. He felt very confident until he saw fat Joe walk in through the rear door, then his courage began to ooze.

"Howdy, Dave! Whutcha want?"

"How yuh, Mistah Joe? Aw, Ah don wanna buy nothing. Ah jus wanted t see of yuhd lemme look at tha ol catlog erwhile."

"Sure! You wanna see it here?"

"Nawsuh. Ah wants t take it home wid me. Ahll bring it back termorrow when Ah come in from the fiels."

"You planning on buyin something?"

"Yessuh."

"Your ma letting you have your own money now?"

"Shucks. Mistah Joe, Ahm gitting t be a man like anybody else! "

Joe laughed and wiped his greasy white face with a red bandanna.

"Whut you plannin on buyin?"

Dave looked at the floor, scratched his head, scratched his thigh, and smiled. Then he looked up shyly.

"Ahll tell yuh, Mistah Joe, ef yuh promise yuh won't tell."

"I promise."

"Waal, Ahma buy a gun."

"A gun? Whut you want with a gun?"

"Ah wanna keep it."

"You ain't nothing but a boy. You don't need a gun."

"Aw, lemme have the catlog, Mistah Joe. Ahll bring it back."

Joe walked through the rear door. Dave was elated. He looked around at barrels of sugar and flour. He heard Joe coming back. He craned his neck to see if he were bringing the book. Yeah, he's got it! Gawddog, he's got it!

"Here, but be sure you bring it back. It's the only one I got."

"Sho, Mistah Joe."

"Say, if you wanna buy a gun, why don't you buy one from me? I gotta gun to sell."

"Will it shoot?"

"Sure it'll shoot."

"Whut kind is it?"

"Oh, it's kinda old . . . A left-hand Wheeler. A pistol. A big one. "

"Is it got bullets in it?"

"It's loaded."

"Kin Ah see it?"

"Where's your money?"

"Whut yuh wan fer it?"

"I'll let you have it for two dollars."

"Just two dollahs? Shucks, Ah could buy tha when Ah git mah pay."

"I will have it here when you want it."

"Awright, suh. Ah be in fer it."

He went through the door, hearing it slam again behind him. Ahma git some money from Ma n buy me a gun! Only two dollahs! He tucked the thick catalogue under his arm and hurried.

"Where yuh been, boy?" His mother held a steaming dish of black-eyed peas.

"Aw, Ma, Ah jus stopped down the road t talk wid th boys."

"Yuh know bettah than t keep suppah waitin."

He sat down, resting the catalogue on the edge of the table.

"Yuh git up from there an git to the well n wash yosef! Ah ain feedin no hogs in mah house!"

She grabbed his shoulder and pushed him. He stumbled out of the room, then came back to get the catalogue.

"Whut this?"

"Aw, Ma, it's jusa catlog."

"Who yuh git it from?"

"From Joe, down at the sto."

"Waal, thas good. We kin use it around the house."

"Naw, Ma." He grabbed for it. "Gimme mah

catlog, Ma."

She held onto it and glared at him.

"Quit hollerin at me! Whut's wrong wid yuh! Yuh crazy?"

"But Ma, please. It ain mine! It's Joe's! He tol me t bring it back t im termorrow."

She gave up the book. He stumbled down the back steps, hugging the thick book under his arm. When he had splashed water on his face and hands, he groped back to the kitchen and fumbled in a corner for the towel. He bumped into a chair; it clattered to the floor. The catalogue sprawled at his feet. When he had dried his eyes he snatched up the book and held it again under his arm. His mother stood watching him.

"Now, ef yuh gona acka fool over that ol book, Ahll take it n burn it up."

"Naw, Ma, please."

"Waal, set down n be still!"

He sat down and drew the oil lamp close. He thumbed page after page, unaware of the food his mother set on the table. His father came in. Then his small brother.

"Whutcha got there, Dave?" his father asked.

"Jusa catlog," he answered, not looking up.

"Ywah, here they is!" His eyes glowed at blue and black revolvers. He glanced up, feeling sudden guilt. His father was watching him. He eased the book under the table and rested it on his knees. After the blessing was asked, he ate. He scooped up peas and swallowed fat meat without chewing. Buttermilk helped to wash it down. He did not want to mention money before his father. He would do much better by cornering his mother when she was alone. He looked at his father uneasily out of the edge of his eye.

"Boy, how come yuh don quit foolin wid tha book n eata yo suppah?"

"Yessuh."

"How you n ol man Hawkins gittin erlong?"

"Suh?"

"Can't yuh hear? Why don yuh lissen? Ah ast you how wuz yuh n old man Hawkins gitting erlong?"

"Oh, swell, Pa. Ah plows mo lan than anybody over there."

"Waal, yuh oughta keep you min on whut yuh doin."

"Yessuh."

He poured his plate full of molasses and sopped at it slowly with a chunk of cornbread. When all but his mother had left the kitchen, he still sat and looked again at the guns in the catalogue. Lawd, ef Ah only had tha pretty one!

He could almost feel the slickness of the weapon with his fingers. If he had a gun like that he would polish it and keep it shining so it would never rust. N Ahd keep it loaded, by Gawd!

"Ma?"

"Hunh?"

"Ol man Hawkins give yuh mah money yit?"

"Yeah, but ain no usa yuh thinkin bout thowin nona it erway. Ahm keepin tha money sos yuh kin have cloes t go to school this winter."

He rose and went to her side with the open catalogue in his palms. She was washing dishes, her head bent low over a pan. Shyly he raised the open book. When he spoke his voice was husky, faint.

"Ma, Gawd knows Ah wans one of these."

"One of whut?" she asked, not raising her eyes.

"One of these," he said again, not daring even to point. She glanced up at the page, then at him with wide eyes.

"Nigger, is yuh gone plum crazy?"

"Aw, Ma– –"

"Git outta here! Don yuh talk t me bout no gun! Yuh a fool!"

"Ma, Ah kin buy one fer two dollahs."

"Not ef Ah knows it yuh ain!"

"But yuh promised me one– –"

"Ah don care whut Ah promised! Yuh ain nothing but a boy yit!"

"Ma, ef yuh lemme buy one Ahll never ast yuh fer nothing no mo."

"Ah tol yuh t git outta here! Yuh ain gonna toucha penny of tha money fer no gun! Thas how come Ah has Mistah Hawkins t pay yo wages t me, cause Ah knows yuh ain got no sense."

"But Ma, we needa gun. Pa ain got no gun. We needa gun in the house. Yuh kin never tell whut might happen."

"Now don yuh try to maka fool outta me, boy! Ef we did have gun yuh wouldn't have it!"

He laid the catalogue down and slipped his arm around her waist.

"Aw, Ma. Ah done worked hard alla summer n ain ast yuh fer nothin, is Ah, now?"

"Thas whut yuh spose t do!"

"But Ma, Ah wans a gun. Yuh kin lemma have two dollahs outa mah money. Please, Ma. I kin give it to Pa . . . Please, Ma! Ah loves yuh, Ma."

When she spoke her voice came soft and low.

"What you wan wida gun, Dave? Yuh don need no gun. Yuhll git in trouble. N ef you Pa just thought Ah let yuh have money t buy a gun he'd hava fit."

"Ahll hide it, Ma. It ain but two dollahs."

"Lawd, chil, whuts wrong wid yuh?"

"Ain nothin wrong, Ma. Alhm almos a man now. Ah wans a gun."

"Who gonna sell yuh a gun?"

"Ol Joe at the sto."

"N it don cos but two dollahs?"

"Thas all, Ma. Just two dollahs. Please, Ma."

She was stacking the plates away; her hands moved slowly, reflectively. Dave kept an anxious silence. Finally, she turned to him.

"Ahll let yuh git tha gun ef yuh promise me one thing"

"Whuts tha, Ma?"

"Yuh bring it straight back t me, yuh hear? It be fer Pa."

"Yesum! Lemme go now, Ma."

She stooped, turned slightly to one side, raised the hem of her dress, rolled down the top of her stocking, and came up with a slender wad of bills.

"Here," she said. "Lawd knows yuh don need no gun. But yer Pa does. Yuh bring it right back t me, yuh hear? Ahma put it up. Now ef yuh don, Ahma have yuh Pa lick yuh so hard yuh won ferget it."

"Yessum."

He took the money, ran down the steps, and across the yard.

"Dave! Yuuuuuh Daaaaave!"

He heard, but he was not going to stop now. "Naw, Lawd!"

The first movement he made the following morning was to reach under his pillow for the gun. In the gray light of dawn he held it loosely, feeling a sense of power. Could killa man wida gun like this. Kill anybody, black or white. And if he were holding his gun in his hand nobody could run over him; they would have to respect him. It was a big gun, with a long barrel and a heavy handle. He raised and lowered it in his hand, marveling at its weight.

He had not come straight home with it as his mother had asked; instead he had stayed out in the fields, holding the weapon in his hand, aiming it now and then at some imaginary foe. But he had not fired it; he had been afraid that his father might hear. Also he was not sure he knew how to fire it.

To avoid surrendering the pistol he had not come into the house until he knew that all were asleep. When his mother had tiptoed to his bedside late that night and demanded the gun, he had first played possum; then he had told her that the gun was hidden outdoors, that he would bring it to her in the morning. Now he lay turning it slowly in his hands. He broke it, took out the cartridges, felt them, and then put them back.

He slid out of bed, got a long strip of old flannel from a trunk, wrapped the gun in it, and tied it to his naked thigh while it was still loaded. He did not go in to breakfast. Even though it was not yet daylight, he started for Jim Hawkins' plantation. Just as the sun was rising he reached the barns where the mules and plows were kept.

"Hey! That you, Dave?"

He turned. Jim Hawkins stood eying him suspiciously.

"What're yuh doing here so early?"

"Ah didn't know Ah wuz gittin up so early, Mistah Hawkins. Ah wuz fixin t hitch up ol Jenny n take her t the fiels."

"Good. Since you're here so early, how about plowing that stretch down by the woods?"

"Suits me, Mistah Hawkins."

"O. K. Go to it!"

He hitched Jenny to a plow and started across the fields. Hot dog! This was just what he wanted. If he could get down by the woods, he could shoot his gun and nobody would hear.

He walked behind the plow, hearing the traces creaking, feeling the gun tied tight to his thigh.

When he reached the woods, he plowed two whole rows before he decided to take out the gun. Finally, he stopped, looked in all directions, then untied the gun and held it in his hand. He turned to the mule and smiled.

"Know whut this is, Jenny? Naw, yuh wouldn't know! Yuhs jusa ol mule! Anyhow, this is a gun, n it kin shoot, by Gawd!"

He held the gun at arm's length. Whut t hell, Ahma shoot this thing! He looked at Jenny again.

"Lissen here, Jenny! When Ah pull this ol trigger Ah don wan yuh t run n acka fool now."

Jenny stood with head down, her short ears pricked straight. Dave walked off about twenty feet, held the gun far out from him, at arm's length, and turned his head. Hell, he told himself, Ah ain afraid. The gun felt loose in his fingers; he waved it wildly for a moment. Then he shut his eyes and tightened his forefinger. Bloom! A report half deafened him and he thought his right hand was torn from his arm. He heard Jenny whinnying and galloping over the field, and he found himself on his knees, squeezing his fingers hard between his legs. His hand was numb; he jammed it into his mouth, trying to warm it, trying to stop the pain. The gun lay at his feet. He did not quite know what had happened. He stood up and stared at the gun as though it were a live thing. He gritted his teeth and kicked the gun. Yuh almos broke mah arm! He turned to look for Jenny; she was far over the fields, tossing her head and kicking wildly.

"Hol on there, ol mule!"

When he caught up with her she stood trembling, walling her big white eyes at him. The plow was far away; the traces had broken. Then Dave stopped short, looking, not believing. Jenny was bleeding. Her left side was red and wet with blood. He went closer. Lawd have mercy! Wondah did Ah shoot this mule? He grabbed for Jenny's mane. She flinched, snorted, whirled, tossing her head.

"Hol on now! Hol on."

Then he saw the hole in Jenny's side, right between the ribs. It was round, wet, red. A crimson stream streaked down the front leg, flowing fast. Good Gawd! Ah wuznt shootin at tha mule. . . . He felt panic. He knew he had to stop that blood, or Jenny would bleed to death. He had never seen so much blood in all his life. He ran the mule for half a mile, trying to catch her. Finally she stopped, breathing hard, stumpy tail half arched. He caught her mane and led her back to where the plow and gun lay. Then he stopped and grabbed handfuls of damp black earth and tried to plug the bullet hole. Jenny shuddered, whinnied, and broke from him.

"Hol on! Hol on now!"

He tried to plug it again, but blood came anyhow. His fingers were hot and sticky. He rubbed dirt hard into his palms, trying to dry them. Then again he attempted to plug the bullet hole, but Jenny shied away, kicking her heels high. He stood helpless. He had to do something. He ran at Jenny; she dodged him. He watched a red stream of blood flow down Jenny's leg and form a bright pool at her feet.

"Jenny . . . Jenny . . ." he called weakly.

His lips trembled. She's bleeding t death! He looked in the direction of home, wanting to go back, wanting to get help. But he saw the pistol lying in the damp black clay. He had a queer feeling that if he only did something, this would not be; Jenny would not be there bleeding to death.

When he went to her this time, she did not move. She stood with sleepy, dreamy eyes; and when he touched her she gave a low-pitched whinny and knelt to the ground, her front knees slopping in blood.

"Jenny . . . Jenny . . ." he whispered.

For a long time she held her neck erect; then her head sank, slowly. Her ribs swelled with a mighty heave and she went over.

Dave's stomach felt empty, very empty. He picked up the gun and held it gingerly between his thumb and forefinger. He buried it at the foot of a tree. He took a stick and tried to cover the pool of blood with dirt—but what was the use? There was Jenny lying with her mouth open and her eyes walled and glassy. He could not tell Jim Hawkins he had shot his mule. But he had to tell something. Yeah, Ahll tell em Jenny started gittin wil n fell on the joint of the plow. . . . But that would hardly happen to a mule. He walked across the field slowly, head down.

It was sunset. Two of Jim Hawkins' men were over near the edge of the woods digging a hole in which to bury Jenny. Dave was surrounded by a knot of people; all of them were looking down at the dead mule.

"I don't see how in the world it happened," said Jim Hawkins for the tenth time.

The crowd parted and Dave's mother, father, and small brother pushed into the center.

"Where Dave?" his mother called.

"There he is," said Jim Hawkins.

His mother grabbed him.

"Whut happened, Dave? Whut yuh done?"

"Nothing."

"C'mon, boy, talk," his father said.

Dave took a deep breath and told the story he knew nobody believed.

"Waal," he drawled. "Ah brung ol Jenny down here sos Ah could do mah plowin. Ah plowed bout two rows, just like yuh see." He stopped and pointed at the long rows of upturned earth. "Then something musta been wrong wid ol Jenny. She wouldn't ack right a-tall. She started snortin n kickin her heels. Ah tried to hol her, but she pulled erway, rearin n goin on. Then when the point of the plow was stickin up in the air, she swung erroun n twisted herself back on it. . . . She stuck herself n started t bleed. N fo Ah could do anything, she wuz dead."

"Did you ever hear of anything like that in all your life?" asked Jim Hawkins.

There were white and black standing in the crowd. They murmured. Dave's mother came close to him and looked hard into his face. "Tell the truth, Dave," she said.

"Looks like a bullet hole ter me," said one man.

"Dave, whut yuh do wid tha gun?" his mother asked.

The crowd surged in, looking at him. He jammed his hands into his pockets, shook his head slowly from left to right, and backed away. His eyes were wide and painful.

"Did he hava gun?" asked Jim Hawkins.

"By Gawd, Ah tol yuh tha wuz a gun wound," said a man, slapping his thigh.

His father caught his shoulders and shook him till his teeth rattled.

"Tell whut happened, yuh rascal! Tell whut . . ."

Dave looked at Jenny's stiff legs and began to cry.

"Whut yuh do wid tha gun?" his mother asked.

"Whut wuz he doin wida gun?" his father asked.

"Come on and tell the truth," said Hawkins. "Ain't nobody going to hurt you . . ."

His mother crowded close to him.

"Did yuh shoot tha mule, Dave?"

Dave cried, seeing blurred white and black faces.

"Ahh ddinnt gggo tt sshoooot hher. . . . Ah ssswear ffo Gawd Ahh ddint. . . . Ah wuz a-trying t sssee ef the ol gggun would sshoot– –"

"Where yuh git the gun from?" his father asked.

"Ah got it from Joe, at the sto."

"Where yuh git the money?"

"Ma give it t me."

"He kept worryin me, Bob. . . . Ah had t. . . . Ah tol im t bring the gun right back t me. . . . It was fer yuh, the gun."

"But how yuh happen to shoot that mule?" asked Jim Hawkins.

"Ah wuznt shootin at the mule, Mistah Hawkins. The gun jumped when Ah pulled the trigger . . . N fo Ah knowed anything Jenny was there a-bleedin."

Somebody in the crowd laughed. Jim Hawkins walked close to Dave and looked into his face.

"Well, looks like you have bought you a mule, Dave."

"Ah swear fo Gawd, Ah didn't go t kill the mule, Mistah Hawkins!"

"But you killed her!"

All the crowd was laughing now. They stood on tiptoe and poked heads over one another's shoulders.

"Well, boy, looks like yuh done bought a dead mule! Hahaha!"

"Ain tha ershame."

"Hohohohoho."

Dave stood, head down, twisting his feet in the dirt.

"Well, you needn't worry about it, Bob," said Jim Hawkins to Dave's father. "Just let the boy keep on working and pay me two dollars a month."

"Whut yuh wan fer yo mule, Mistah Hawkins?"

Jim Hawkins screwed up his eyes.

"Fifty dollars."

"Whut yuh do wid tha gun?" Dave's father demanded.

Dave said nothing.

"Yuh wan me t take a tree lim n beat yuh till yuh talk!"

"Nawsuh!"

"Whut yuh do wid it?"

"Ah thowed it erway."

"Where?"

"Ah. . . Ah thowed it in the creek."

"Waal, c mon home. N firs thing in the mawnin git to tha creek n fin tha gun."

"Yessuh."

"What yuh pay fer it?"

"Two dollahs."

"Take tha gun n git you money back n carry it t Mistah Hawkins, yuh hear? N don fergit

Ahma lam you black bottom good fer this! Now march yosef on home, suh!"

Dave turned and walked slowly. He heard people laughing. Dave glared, his eyes welling with tears. Hot anger bubbled in him. Then he swallowed and stumbled on.

That night Dave did not sleep. He was glad that he had gotten out of killing the mule so easily, but he was hurt. Something hot seemed to turn over inside him each time he remembered how they had laughed. He tossed on his bed, feeling his hard pillow. N Pa says he's gonna beat me. . . . He remembered other beatings, and his back quivered. Naw, naw, Ah sho don want im t beat me tha way no mo. . . . Dam em all. Nobody ever gave him anything. All he did was work. They treat me like a mule.. . . N then they beat me.. . . He gritted his teeth. N Ma had t tell on me.

Well, if he had to, he would take old man Hawkins that two dollars. But that meant selling the gun. And he wanted to keep that gun. Fifty dollahs fer a dead mule.

He turned over, thinking how he had fired the gun. He had an itch to fire it again. Ef other men kin shoota gun, by Gawd, Ah kin! He was still listening. Mebbe they all sleepin now. . . . The house was still. He heard the soft breathing of his brother. Yes, now! He would go down and get that gun and see if he could fire it! He eased out of bed and slipped into overalls.

The moon was bright. He ran almost all the way to the edge of the woods. He stumbled over the ground, looking for the spot where he had buried the gun. Yeah, here it is. Like a hungry dog scratching for a bone he pawed it up. He puffed his black cheeks and blew dirt from the trigger and barrel. He broke it and found four cartridges unshot. He looked around; the fields were filled with silence and moonlight. He clutched the gun stiff and hard in his fingers. But as soon as he wanted to pull the trigger, he shut his eyes and turned his head. Naw, Ah can't shoot wid mah eyes closed n mah head turned. With effort he held his eyes open: then he squeezed. Blooooom! He was stiff, not breathing. The gun was still in his hands. Dammit, he'd done it! He fired again. Blooooom! He smiled. Blooooom! Blooooom! Click, click. There! It was empty. If anybody could shoot a gun, he could. He put the gun into his hip pocket and started across the fields.

When he reached the top of a ridge he stood straight and proud in the moonlight, looking at Jim Hawkins' big white house, feeling the gun sagging in his pocket. Lawd, ef Ah had jus one mo bullet Ahd taka shot at tha house. Ahd like t scare ol man Hawkins jusa little. . . . Jusa enough t let im know Dave Sanders is a man.

To his left the road curved, running to the tracks of the Illinois Central. He jerked his head, listening. From far off came a faint hoooof-hoooof; hoooof-hoooof; hoooof-hoooof . . . That's number eight. He took a swift look at Jim Hawkins' white house; he thought of Pa, of Ma, of his little brother, and the boys. He thought of the dead mule and heard hoooof-hoooof; hoooof-hoooof; hoooof-hoooof . . . He stood rigid. Two dollahs a mont. Les see now. . . Tha means itll take bout two years. Shucks! Ahll be dam!

He started down the road, toward the tracks. Yeah, here she comes! He stood beside the track and held himself stiffly. Here she comes, erroun the ben. . . . C mon, yuh slowpoke! C mon! He had his hand on his gun; something quivered in his stomach. Then the train thundered past, the gray and brown boxcars rumbling and clinking. He gripped the gun tightly; then he jerked his hand out of his pocket. Ah betcha Bill wouldn't do it! Ah betcha. . . . The cars slid past, steel grinding upon steel. Ahm riding yuh ternight so hep me

Gawd! He was hot all over. He hesitated just a moment; then he grabbed, pulled atop of a car, and lay flat. He felt his pocket; the gun was still there. Ahead the long rails were glinting in moonlight, stretching away, away to somewhere, somewhere where he could be a man. . . .

I. THE STORY LINE

A. Digging for Facts

1. Dave wants a gun because he (a) is afraid of the other field hands, (b) is determined to leave home, (c) has a score to settle with Mr. Hawkins, (d) believes a gun will make him a man.

2. Although Joe thinks Dave is too young to have a gun, he (a) agrees that perhaps Dave would feel safer with a gun, (b) advises Dave to buy a small pistol, (c) loans Dave the Sears catalog, (d) offers to teach Dave how to shoot.

3. Dave approaches his mother about buying a gun because (a) she also wishes there were a gun in the house, (b) he knows his father, if asked, would never agree, (c) she is free with her money, (d) he and his father are not speaking.

4. Mrs. Sanders agrees to let Dave have the two dollars on one condition, that he (a) never bring the gun in the house, (b) keep the gun out of his younger brother's reach, (c) promise not to tell where he got the money, (d) give the gun to her immediately.

5. To avoid surrendering his gun Dave (a) claims Joe would not sell it after all, (b) says he gave it to his father, (c) tells his mother the gun is hidden outside, (d) goes straight from Joe's store to work.

6. Once out in the fields, Dave (a) rushes to show off his new gun, (b) abandons his work and goes hunting, (c) warns Jenny not to run off, (d) hides the gun for future use.

7. Seeing the hole in Jenny's side, Dave (a) screams for help, (b) tries to plug the wound with dirt, (c) decides to run away to avoid punishment, (d) vows never to use the gun again.

8. According to Dave, Jenny's wound was caused by (a) a stray bullet shot from the woods, (b) a fall she took while struggling over rough ground, (c) his own wild practice shot, (d) the point of the plow.

9. After Mr. Hawkins learns the truth, he (a) sells the mule to Dave, (b) threatens to turn Dave over to the authorities, (c) docks the pay of each member of Dave's family, (d) has Dave beaten and turned off his land.

10. Rather than be punished, Dave hops a train headed for (a) a place where he can be a man, (b) Illinois and the biggest city he can find, (c) the only other place he has been, Charlotte, (d) the North and freedom.

B. Probing for Theme

Richard Wright wrote about life as he knew it, and his stories, like life, do not necessarily center on an easily identifiable theme or message. Often after reading one of Wright's stories, the reader is left to judge for him or herself what the story was all about. (Wright tries to tell the truth and the reader must draw his or her own conclusions.)

Look at the following statements. Which statement most closely approximates what you think Wright was trying to say in "Almos' a Man"?

1. Growing up is a long and difficult process.
2. A boy becomes a man when he starts acting like one.

3. Sometimes running away is the only way to prove one's independence.
4. A boy will never become a man if others continue to treat him like a child.

What specific incidents lead you to your conclusion about the story's meaning?

Perhaps none of these statements express what you think is the main point of the story. If that is the case, write a sentence which states what you think the story is all about.

II. IN SEARCH OF MEANING

1. Why does Dave want a gun? What does the gun represent to him? What reasons does Dave give to Joe for wanting to own a gun?

2. Why does Dave talk to his mother rather than his father about buying a gun? What argument does Dave use to persuade his mother to let him have a gun? What does this argument reveal about Dave's real reasons for wanting a gun?
3. After Dave has the gun, what does he do with it? What does his behavior reveal about him? Is he really ready to accept responsibility for his own actions?
4. Describe briefly Dave's first attempt to fire the gun. How does Dave react when he discovers the hole in Jenny's side? What does Dave's explanation of the mule's death reveal about him?
5. How does Dave respond to his punishment? What does his response reveal about him? Is Dave really a man?

III. DEVELOPING WORD POWER

Exercise A

Below are some words that may not have been clear to you when you read the story. You will see each word in its original context followed by four possible choices. From the four choices, select the one which best defines the word as it appears in the story.

1. to grope

   " . . ., he *groped* back to the kitchen and fumbled in a corner for the towel."

   a. to rush angrily
   b. to feel about uncertainly
   c. to proceed hastily
   d. to move impatiently

2. possum

   ". . . had first played *possum*;"

   a. to act dumb
   b. to act foolish
   c. to act sick
   d. to act asleep

3. to flinch

   "She *flinched*, snorted, whirled, tossing her head."

   a. to withdraw fearfully
   b. to charge wildly
   c. to turn suddenly
   d. to shake uncontrollably

4. surged
   "The crowd *surged* in, . . ."
   a. walked
   b. hesitated
   c. rushed
   d. shoved

5. quivered
   " . . . and his back *quivered*."
   a. itched
   b. stung
   c. ached
   d. trembled

Exercise B

From the list of vocabulary words at the beginning of this exercise, choose a word which best completes each of the following sentences.

a.ooze
b. elated
c. reflectively
d. traces
e. gingerly
f. groped
g. possum
h. flinched
i. surged
j. quivered

1. No amount of struggling could free the wild stallion from the _?_ the cowpokes had attached.
2. After the initial shock of seeing the champion defeated, the fans _?_ in towards the ring for a closer look.
3. Gazing _?_ at the fire, the old man seemed to recall rather than feel the heat of the flames.
4. The eager puppy _?_ in anticipation of the touch of his owner's gentle hand.
5. As the child watched her classmates receive their shots, she _?_ as if she felt their pain.
6. The surgeon _?_ probed the patient's stomach for signs of internal injury.
7. Nothing could persuade the grieving child that her kitten was not just playing _?_.
8. _?_ by his team's recent victory, the quarterback ached for a chance to play in the league playoffs.
9. Blinded by the glare of a thousand flashbulbs, the singer _?_ his way off stage.

10. According to first reports from the new drilling site, oil practically _?_ up out of the ground.

IV. IMPROVING WRITING SKILLS

Exercise A

Richard Wright uses adjectives and adverbs sparingly in "Almos' a Man." Instead, he relies on carefully selected verbs to convey visually his characters' state of mind. Look at the following exerpt from the story. Pay careful attention to the verbs and verb phrases Wright has used.

> "She gave up the book. He stumbled down the back steps, hugging the thick book under his arm. When he had splashed water on his face and hands, he groped back to the kitchen and fumbled in a corner for the towel. He bumped into a chair; it clattered to the floor. The catalogue sprawled at his feet. When he had dried his eyes he snatched up the book and held it again under his arm."

What impression of Dave do you get while reading this passage? How do Wright's verb choices contribute to that impression?

Using different verbs, try to create an image of Dave which is more relaxed and graceful.

> She ____ the book. He ____ down the back steps, ____ the thick book under his arm. When he had ____ water on his face and hands, he ____ to the kitchen and ____ in a corner for the towel. He ____ into a chair; it ____ to the floor. The catalogue ____ at his feet. When he ____ his eyes he ____ up the book and ____ it again under his arm.

Exercise B

Writers frequently break rules of grammar, punctuation, and proper usage when writing dialogue or expressing a character's thoughts. Often nonstandard English is substituted as well. Look at the following passage from

"Almos 'a Man." Then rewrite it in standard English applying the rules of proper grammar, punctuation, and usage.

> "Dave struck out across the fields, looking homeward through paling light. Whut's the usa talking wid em niggers in the field? Anyhow, his mother was putting supper on the table. Them niggers can't understan nothing. One of these days he was going to get a gun and practice shooting, then they can't talk to him as though he were a little boy. He slowed, looking at the ground. Shucks, Ah ain scareda them even ef they are biggern me! Aw, Ah know whut Ahma do. . . . Ahm going by ol Joe's sto n git that Sears Roebuck catlog n look at them guns. Mabbe Ma will lemme buy one when she gits mah pay from ol man Hawkins. Ahma beg her t gimme some money. Ahm ol ernough to hava gun. Ahm seventeen. Almost a man. He strode, felling his long, loose-joint limbs. Shucks, a man oughta hava little gun aftah he done worked hard all day. . . ."

How does your version differ from the original? Which version is more effective? Why?

V. THINGS TO WRITE OR TALK ABOUT

1. In several places within the story, Dave offers different reasons for wanting to have a gun. What are some of those reasons? Why is owning a gun really so important to Dave? What does the gun symbolize to Dave?

2. According to Wright, ". . . to tell the truth is the hardest thing on earth. . ." Yet in his writing he strives to tell of life as it really is. What is the truth Wright is trying to reveal in "Almos' a Man"? Write a brief essay answering this question. Be sure to cite examples to support your thesis.

3. In many ways Dave's position, caught between boyhood and manhood, parallels that of every adolescent approaching adulthood. Dave is seventeen, fully grown, and doing a man's job. Why then is he still only almos' a man? Cite examples from the story to support your position.

4. What qualities does Dave associate with being a man? Do you agree or disagree with Dave's view of manhood? In a short essay summarize your views on what it means to be a man or a woman.

5. Richard Wright is a realist, not a romantic. His stories rarely present idealized heroes and a happy ending is never guaranteed. His stories tell of life as it is, not as it ought to be, yet they are rarely without a message. What seems to be the central message of "Almos' a Man"? Use examples to support your position.

ANSWER KEY

I. THE STORY LINE

A. Digging for Facts

1. d	3. b	5. c	7. b	9. a
2. c	4. d	6. c	8. d	10. a

B. Probing for Theme

Support could be given for both statements 1 and 2. While Dave does run away, statement 3 is not supported by the title. Statement 4 reflects, in part, Dave's feelings, but not the truth of the story.

III. DEVELOPING WORD POWER

Exercise A

1. to grope
   b. to feel about uncertainly
2. possum
   d. to act asleep
3. to flinch
   a. to withdraw fearfully
4. surged
   c. rushed
5. quivered
   d. trembled

Exercise B

1. (d) traces
2. (i) surged
3. (c) reflectively
4. (j) quivered
5. (h) flinched
6. (e) gingerly
7. (g) possum
8. (b) elated
9. (f) groped
10. (a) oozed